The Book of Life

A TALE OF TWO FRIENDS

Adapted by Ellie O' Ryan

Illustrated by Tom Caulfield, Frederick Gardner, Megan Petasky, and Allen Tam

Ready-to-Read

Simon Spotlight

New York   London   Toronto   Sydney   New Delhi

SIMON SPOTLIGHT
An imprint of Simon & Schuster Children's Publishing Division
1230 Avenue of the Americas, New York, New York 10020
First Simon Spotlight edition September 2014
THE BOOK OF LIFE © 2014 Twentieth Century Fox Film Corporation and Reel FX Productions II, LLC. All rights reserved.
All rights reserved, including the right of reproduction in whole or in part in any form.
SIMON SPOTLIGHT, READY-TO-READ, and colophon are registered trademarks of Simon & Schuster, Inc.
For information about special discounts for bulk purchases, please contact Simon & Schuster Special Sales at 1-866-506-1949
or business@simonandschuster.com.
Manufactured in the United States of America 0814 LAK
2 4 6 8 10 9 7 5 3 1
ISBN 978-1-4814-2574-2 (hc)
ISBN 978-1-4814-2573-5 (pbk)
ISBN 978-1-4814-2575-9 (eBook)

This is the town of San Angel.
Two boys, Manolo and Joaquin,
live here.
They aren't just friends.
They are best friends.

Joaquin and Manolo have big dreams.
Joaquin wants to be a hero,
just like his father.

Manolo hopes to be a musician.
But his father wants him to be
a famous bullfighter.

Big dreams aren't all that Manolo
and Joaquin have in common.
They even like the same girl.
Her name is Maria.
The two friends would do
anything for her.

One day, Joaquin meets
a strange old man.
The man gives
Joaquin a special present:
the Medal of Everlasting Life.

The person who wears the medal cannot be hurt.
Now nothing will stop Joaquin from becoming a hero like his dad!

The next day, Joaquin, Manolo, and Maria
are playing in the market.
When Maria sees pigs in a stable
next to a butcher shop, she feels
so sorry for them.
She comes up with a plan to free
the animals.

Will Manolo and Joaquin help her?
Of course!
Maria hits the lock with a sword.
"Freedom is coming through!"
she cries.

Uh-oh! The pigs are running wild!
Everyone in San Angel is scared,
even Maria's father, General Posada.

When a big warthog charges at him,
Manolo and Joaquin know what to do.
"No retreat?" Joaquin yells.
"No surrender!" Manolo yells back.

Joaquin pushes General Posada
to safety.
Wham! The warthog hits Joaquin!
But thanks to the Medal of
Everlasting Life, Joaquin is fine.

Then Manolo grabs a red cape.
Swish, swish!
He swings it through the air,
leading the warthog away.
Manolo and Joaquin are both heroes.
But General Posada only pays
attention to Joaquin.

General Posada is angry with
Maria for letting the pigs loose.
He decides to send her to
a school far away.
General Posada hopes that
Maria will learn to behave better
while she is gone.

Manolo and Joaquin watch as the
train takes Maria away.
They have never felt so sad.

Many years pass. Joaquin becomes
the hero of San Angel, thanks to
his special medal.

Manolo stays busy too. He plays guitar every day. He also practices his bullfighting moves.

But the friends never stop missing Maria.

At last, Maria comes home!
Joaquin knows that Maria will love
his medals.
Manolo wants to impress Maria
with his music.
But his dad has planned
Manolo's first bullfight for that day.

Instead of fighting the bull,
Manolo would rather play a song.
"Hurting the bull is wrong!"
Manolo yells from the ring.
The whole town boos him.
But Manolo knows that he did the
right thing. And so does Maria.

At General Posada's house,
Joaquin shows Maria
all the medals he won in battle.
Maria is bored.
Joaquin only wants to talk
about himself!

Manolo comes to see Maria
later that night.
When Manolo sings to Maria,
they fall in love.

But it is too late.
General Posada wants
Joaquin to marry Maria.
"What are you going to do?"
Joaquin asks Manolo.

Joaquin and Manolo have a big fight.
They don't feel like friends anymore.
Especially not best friends.

Then something terrible happens.
A group of bandits attack
San Angel!

Their leader, Chakal,
wants to steal everything,
including the Medal of
Everlasting Life.
If Chakal gets the medal, he will be
unstoppable.

Joaquin is ready to be a hero.

He fights bravely.

But Chakal and his men threaten Maria and her father!

Joaquin needs to give the medal to Chakal to save them.

Just in time, Manolo jumps in!
He's ready to battle the bandits.
Maria grabs a sword too.
But Chakal is really big . . .
and really bad.
He wants to destroy the town!

The friends know that it's time
to defeat Chakal once and for all.
Joaquin knows this is
his chance to prove
that he really is a hero.

Joaquin grabs Manolo and gives him
the Medal of Everlasting Life.
Now Manolo won't get hurt while
he fights Chakal.
"No retreat?" says Manolo.

"No surrender!" Joaquin replies.
Because that is what a true hero—
and a true friend—
would do.